Belinda Blinked 4;

Author: Rocky Flintstone;

An erotic story of sexual prowess, sexy characters and even bigger business deals whilst the darkness increases;

Keep following the sexiest sales girl in business as she continues to earn her big, huge bonus by being the best at removing her tight silken stockings.

The short bit;

From Rocky Flintstone, the self published author who put the 'rot' in Erotica, the 4th book of the Belinda Blinked series leaves the faithful reader again gasping for oxygen as treason threatens the very fabric of our world. Belinda Blinked 3 ended in high suspense as super villain, Herr Wolfgang Bisch, exposed his plans to dominate the world of Pots and Pans, taking Belinda's company down in the process. But, Belinda has set a blistering pace and her customers are unrelenting, they need Belinda to be on top of her game as they continue to order more and more of the products they so love from their favourite International Sales Director. After all, a pot is a pot and a pan is a pan... so why not buy them from the best?

Yes, great sex, betrayal, large breasts and hotel room chatter, never mind the odd bottle of Australian Chardonnay, a Gin and Tonic and even better consensual sex all come together to give you... faithful reader, a sexually charged atmospheric ride through Belinda Blinked 4.... You've been warned!

Contents;

Chapter 1;

Dearly Beloved;

Belinda Blinked;

She must have nodded off. Hard to do on one leg. After all it was a rainy Friday afternoon. She shook her head as the tenth pair of frilly French knickers scraped down her long legs. She scooped them up and put them on the stack of used underwear sitting on her desk.

One by one she set to work, stuffing one at a time into a jiffy bag complete with the latest Steele's Pots and Pans rate card. She licked every envelope closed and triple checked the addresses. Peter Rouse, Claus Bloch, Alfonse Stirbacker, Jim Stirling etc;

Satisfied she piled them into her out tray and called to reception.

'Maeve, these are ready to be posted out please.'

Belinda swivelled on her chrome casters. She was bored, oh so bored with paperwork. She'd been hard at it for a whole two days now determined to clear her desk before Giselle and Tony's wedding on Saturday.

Fast forward and Belinda Blumenthal was humming to herself in her large bathtub smothered in soap suds up to her ear holes. The early morning sun glinted off St. Paul's Cathedral and penetrated her penthouse apartment bathroom. Leaning back she relaxed taking care to not splash soapy water over the expensive Thailand forest mahogany floor she'd just had recently fitted.

Suddenly her body tensed and twitched as if she'd been stung by a vicious ant. Chiara Montague's submerged head bobbed above the suds, gasping for both air and penance.

'Oh my god, Belinda, did I nuzzle you too sharply?' she gurgled. 'I'm sooooo sorry darling.'

'It's fine Chiara, but I have no desire to be chewed to pieces on this wedding day of all days. Come sugar puff, I'll put the kettle on.'

As Belinda stood up, the soapy bubbles cascaded down her curved back and over her long legs, where they gushed a streaming chute into the water below. Belinda tightened her bathrobe around herself making sure her ample breasts were covered and went to put the kettle on. She knew it would take five minutes to boil.

'Nice pad babe.' Chiara purred as her practised eye followed the London skyline stretching out all around the building.

The dress Chiara had designed exclusively for Belinda was heaven on a hat stand. Sequinned gold, it pushed her tits up to her chin and the lugubrious slit up the leg was as classy as it was practical. A wedding was always a good opportunity to make new business contacts and Belinda, dressed as she was to die for, was, now all set. Miss Montague's multi-million-pound-worthy hands sewed the Steele's Pots and Pans International Sales Director into her skin tight dress with a final stitch. As the final touches were made to the hem, Belinda got an electric shock. Was it static from the dress or Chiara being naughty… you could never tell with these public school types.

Just then, Belinda had the urge to kiss her seamstress but Chiara's mouth was full of pins. No matter, Belinda had to be off and for once there was no time for yet more hanky panky.

'I'm sorry you can't be my twenty-first-century date like we discussed Chiara, but they've been frugal with plus ones.'

In a very lovely flowery frock with shoulder puffs Chiara looked crestfallen and the smallest of salt tears crept from her left eye.

'Just close the door on your way out. Or wait for my drunken ass to return in the early hours.' Belinda winked as she slammed the double padlocked fire door shut.

Belinda parked her Jaguar in the last available space in the very large Church carpark.

'Good God,' she thought, and then remembered she was on hallowed ground, 'Sorry God, but I didn't really think so many people would be here.' God nodded, even he was surprised if truth be told.

Belinda walked up the aisle, feeling like Penelope Tree. She sensed eye upon eye upon eye focusing on her jiggling ass. Eyes of those she loved and eyes of those she had yet to love. At the front of the church Belinda noticed an older woman very similar to Giselle, but without the shorn hair styling. It must be her sex-starved Dutch/Belgian mother she mused.

On the other side of the aisle was a tall man, with a brusque moustache and no companion to speak of. It had to be Tony's dad. Like his son he was ex-army and someone you didn't tangle with. She'd heard Tony's Mum had succumbed to yellow fever years ago when they were all posted overseas.

Bella beckoned her into the empty seat next to her. She looked stunning piled into a white evening gown. The rhinestone jewellery was particularly eye catching Belinda thought when Giselle, on the arm of a strange man, passed by her.

The bride slowly made her way up to the altar, her large nipples quivering at the sound of the bass notes in Handel's masterpiece. Giselle knew this was her day; she'd worked months, no years, to achieve this result.

As she greeted Tony at the altar; handsomely dressed in his finest clothes, Bella turned and half shouted

'Belinda, I think this is the happiest day of my life.'

'There, there, dearest Bella. Every dog has its day.' Belinda whispered as she positioned her hand over her colleague's crotch. It went from a pat to a dab to a full on caress. It wasn't long before Bella had mucus emitting from every hole. Tears from her eye-ducks; snot from her nose and divine juices from her labia.

'Dearly beloved,' the Vicar droned on, 'We are gathered here today to witness the marriage of Tony Sylvester and Giselle Maarschalkerweerd de Klotz of Steele's Pots and Pans. Blah, blah, blah, Belinda's mind interrupted. Nothing beats the efficiency of a registry office she joked with herself. It took all her refinement to not burst out laughing.

As the congregation wept and grinned, a slight figure under a big hat and long morning coat snuck as quietly as he could into the back of the empty church. In between the short hymns you could just discern the sound of his wooden bamboo cane tapping on the cold, stone floor.

Belinda secretively craned her head to either side and then back for confirmation of her suspicion. The figure, coughing a silent hoarse cough, slowly inched his way to a wooden pew behind a large stone pillar tucked away from view.

Perspiring freely, the phantom sat down, exhausted. The ten minute walk, no crawl, from the carpark had nearly done for him. But he knew he had to be there.

'Hang on' Belinda thought. 'That could not possibly be… He wouldn't dare…Surely…'

'Dearly beloved,' the vicar continued, 'If anyone has anything to say why these two people should not be married…'

Belinda Blinked;

Chapter 2;

Tony's Secret;

The organ growled out its duty, the church bells rang and Tony and Giselle left the church with a new symbiotic relationship the world called marriage. But to Giselle it was just another step in her life plan. Outside the large wooden front doors the Steele's Pots and Pans Senior Sales Team held up a series of Oxy Brillo pots and pans in a triumphal arch. Tony and Giselle walked slowly under it kissing each other inappropriately. Tony's left hand was already firmly planted in Giselle's buttocks and as cheers of much happiness for the future emanated from the guests, the happy couple climbed into their wedding car and were whisked away to the reception being held at Sir James Godwin's mansion near Windsor.

Bella by now had a wet stain over her crotch making her white dress somewhat see-through. She caught Belinda by the arm and said,

'Will I ever be a Mrs do you think Belinda? Is this day on the cards for me one day?'

Belinda wasn't listening. Her head was already puzzling over who she thought she'd spied in the church. She nodded at the damp Bella and made for her car. She needed a good stiff gin and tonic, and fast.

At the reception building guests drank the sparkling Australian Chardonnay freely. Belinda had found herself in a gossip bubble with Bella, the Countess Zara of Leningrad and the Russian devil Grigor Calanski.

'Where is that spunky little leprechaun on the switchboard?' growled Grigor. 'I call her Irish.'

'Who Maeve on reception?' replied Belinda in a hush. 'She wasn't invited.'

'Vy?' asked the Countess from under her enormous double rimmed firecracker of a hat.

'Tony doesn't trust her,' interrupted Bella in between bites of whole mini toad in the holes, 'he thinks she's not Kosher.'

Zara's one visible eye sparkled.

'I saw her on Skype vonce. She looked shifty. A perfect fit for my loose ladies of darkness. I tried to poach the little kitten tail, I promised her riches and spice but she said she refused to budge her little sexy ass.'

'I don't know if Bella's telling the truth. Tony hired her after all.' remarked Belinda sagely.

Bella blew a wet raspberry. A little spittle landed on the old dog Calanski's thick top lip which he slobbered up greedily.

Belinda continued,

'The reality is, Grigor, and you aren't to know this being an expert in caviar and not pots and pans, but she has to man the phones back at Steele's HQ. After all, the world of the second largest supplier of quality cookware in Europe never sleeps.'

'You are too trusting English!' grinned the Soviet svelte.

Just then the obviously physical wreck of a man from the church approached the happy couple at the top table. Again Belinda had to admit he was vaguely familiar but still couldn't place him. Noticing the man, Tony shook his head in total disbelief. It couldn't be, it was impossible;

he'd been reported dead for over six years now. But deep down Tony knew it... it was unbelievably his long lost brother.

'Geooorrggge!' Tony shouted and ran to hold his physically broken younger brother in his arms.

Lieutenant George Sylvester; retired SAS and until six years ago a senior black-ops operative with GreenSword Global Corporation, had been a mercenary for hire operating out of the Arabian Gulf. Tough and extremely capable he was known as a man. Whilst admittedly still young, who would take no shit from anyone and was acknowledged as the ultimate craftsman in his chosen field of penetrative insurgence.

'Who iz thiz cripple thing?' spat the Countess Zara replicating the general thinking of the guest list en mass.

'George... is it you... you're alive?'

Tony turned round to his father and shouted, 'Father, come here, quickly... it's your son, my brother and Giselle's brother in law George returned to us by some matrimonial miracle!'

The room erupted in applause mixed with mirth... and some pity at his limping form. Tony's father, Colonel Reginald Anthony George Sylvester strode across the room shaking his head... tears rolling down his cheeks. The three men clutched each other in a quiet celebration of living life and sobbed for unbelievable joy.

Belinda Blinked;

Belinda knew she'd seen him somewhere, an old black and white photograph on Tony's desk... 'How nice he's not really dead.' she thought.

Belinda politely excused herself because she needed the loo. In her experience, happiness moved the bowls as much as the heart. As she sashayed down the rambling varnished hallway floorboards to the powder room, Belinda tripped over a genuine snakeskin cowboy boot.

'Giddy up, missy.' said a familiar voice.

Belinda swivelled on her belly like a lost fish washed upon the seashore.

'Jim Stirling!' she gushed.

'Eat me' he replied.

Belinda carefully unzipped Jim's Leevee's as quickly as she could in her half-delirious state. She carefully inspected his appendage wondering how the toll of time and use had aged it. She needed not have worried; Marco Ourigues had indeed created a monument to womankind meant to last. Belinda greedily engulfed Jim's rising penis in her mouth. He grabbed her tits but was being frustrated by Chiara Montagues final stitches.

'Gee, Belinder, this dress of yours is some fine fit, how da ya get out of it?'

Belinda struggled to answer through her cock stuffed mouth.

'Jim, stop messing about, just fuck me hard... tear the fucking dress off with those massive hands...and thumbs...'

Jim needed no further bidding and Belinda shed her dress as a lizard would shed its scales. She sat on top of his king sized cock, fucking him for all she was worth.

'Oh how she did enjoy being back in Texas... Yeee Haaa!'

With the might of an Olympic rower Jim pulled Belinda towards him and back; towards him and back, towards him and back until it became clear he was going to offload his essence all over the matt varnished floorboards.

'I'm gonna cum.' he grunted.

'Not in me you're not, Sunny Jim, I have a whole day to enjoy yet.' said Belinda as she hopped off his pumping penis (jolly sausage).

The eruption started in Jim's monstrous testicles, travelled through his vas deferens and thundered along his urethra into his throbbing cock whence he ejaculated a powerful surge. Luckily, Belinda had the reactions of a bobcat and managed to duck just in the nick of time. She watched as his teal coloured super sauce surged over her head and splattered over the three tiered wedding gateaux unluckily positioned behind her ass.

'Shit!' gasped the knackered tycoon.

They both looked at the cake, dripping in 250 million flicks of blue seamen.

'I think it's quite snazzy,' mused Belinda, 'I've seen similar things at the Tate Modern. Wipe yourself clean Jim, and see you on the dance floor... big boy!'

With that, Belinda threw a tablecloth over her naked body, wiggled her bum cheeks and sashayed back to the wedding reception party.

Jim Stirling Blinked;

Chapter 3;

Cubical confessions;

Belinda Blumenthal slinked into her seat carefully tucking her designer white linen sheet around her sexual body just as Sir James was wrapping up his Best Man's Speech.

'So in conclusion I'd like to thank all the hangers on…. bridesmaids; ushers; etc;' Sir James bowed, curtseyed and bowed again.

'But… and this needs to be said, as you all know, Tony and Giselle are two very key members of the Steele's Pots and Pans organisation. Without them Pot sales wouldn't be up by an amazing 550%. Griddles wouldn't be up 327%. And don't even get me started on the braisier pans.'

Belinda whistled through her clenched teeth, all this talk of pans was making her labia gently sweat with pre-cum.

'And to be sure all the food we are consuming today has been prepared on our very fine quality, yet affordable cookware…'

Tony whispered to his new beloved,

'He's doing a dry run of his AGM speech next week, the cheeky old bugger.' Giselle grinned through the divine shaved lime pie she was tucking into.

'But we do have to accept the competition is fierce,' continued Sir James, 'our opposition, especially Bicsh Hestellerung based in East Berlin, show us no mercy.'

Suddenly, at the mention of Bisch, Bella coughed into her champagne flute. Bubbles popped out of her nose as she tried to regain the poise she had so conspicuously lost. Belinda threw her a suspicious side-eye shadiness of the highest degree.

'However our Oxy Brillo range is performing magnificently...'

The room erupted in cheers.

'Hrrrmmmph, Ladies and Gentlemen, please recharge your glasses...'

'The Bride the Groom!'

The Skillet Table toasted the happy couple and chatted about the economic situation in general. Everyone agreed that the larger economies were tightening up, much like Bella's vagina Grigor thought wistfully. Over on The Casserole Pot Table Dr. Robbins and Helga, now seemingly an item, were deep in conversation with the Rouses... Belinda kept hearing strange Dutch phrases wafting across the room.

It wasn't long before Belinda had managed to get a jive with Dr. Robbins on the cards; well Belinda was dancing, Dr. Robbins was just slowly gyrating from leg to leg with a delicate little hop thrown in every few seconds.

'I love this world we live in.' Dr Robbins said in a voice quickly rising to falsetto level.

Belinda winced. She couldn't help but laugh, the man... if he was a man, was surely nuts, but just then the beautiful Helga grabbed her arm.

'Belinda' Helga shouted at her... 'I need to talk to you urgently.'

'Of course Helga. Ladies toilets?' replied Belinda.

Luckily Helga understood the word toilet, as it was pretty similar to the Dutch which was also toilet.

The girls left the good Doctor rocking from foot to foot, nodding his head incessantly, to a tune only he could imagine or hear.

In the outer WC's, the delicious Helga pulled Belinda into a cubicle. It was larger than average with very pretty tiled cornicing around the edge. It was pink, one of Belinda's new fav colours. Helga slammed the door shut.

'Strip me Belinda, fuck me Belinda, everything is not as it seems Belinda!'

Belinda pulled the fabulous fleece cocktail dress from Helga's willing body. Helga lost no time in pushing her hot crotch into Belinda's cool thigh.

A powerful spark jumped between them.

"Oohh." said Belinda.

"Aahhh." replied Helga.

Helga quickly stripped the white designer sheet off Belinda, who underneath was already totally naked, and found her mouth with her tongue. Slowly, slowly, ever so slowly Helga brought the pulsating Belinda under her Dutchland spell. Helga's licking utensil started to massage her juddering clitoris intensely.

Suddenly she stopped dead.

'Belinda… Belinda, listen to me,' Helga gasped in fluent English with the hint of yank. 'I'm really sorry but I have to give you this bad news…'

Helga squeezed Belinda's tits against her head, creating a breast face sandwich. She continued her sexual advance with aplomb. In fact she was unstoppable, woman and machine combined into the most potent adversary Belinda had ever encountered. Belinda sucked in all the air….

Helga stopped again;

'It's really important that you can't tell a soul. Not a man, not a woman. Not even your pet parrot.'

Belinda couldn't believe it. How did Helga know about Chi Chi?? It made no sense.

Helga whisked Belinda's clit with her right handed forefinger. Belinda swooned and lost all feeling between her calves and toes. She collapsed. But Helga mercifully managed to catch her just before her head hit the pink ceramic toilet cistern.

Helga spoke directly into Belinda.

'You're the only one I can trust with this information. Do you get it? Tell me you get it!'

But Belinda didn't get it. Helga once more upped the sexual pressure cooker of lust. At long last both girls could no longer deny nature and they orgasmed in a series of ear splitting screams which must have reached the boogying next door.

'Right. Listen carefully.' Helga panted.

Looking around the locked, empty cubicle for nosey parkers, Helga pushed the chrome handle down causing the rhapsodic flush to fill the room with a loud tinkling water noise.

Helga said something. But Belinda didn't catch it. The flush was too loud for her sensitive little ears.

Belinda shook her head whilst Helga fumed.

'Ah Gad... Listeeeennnnn. I'm F.B.I.' whispered Helga.

Belinda Blinked;

Belinda stopped in mid motion....had she understood correctly? She knew Helga wasn't the best English speaker in Holland, but FBI? Helga made a strange burbling noise as Belinda found her clit with her tongue, FBI or not, Belinda would do SP&P justice when it came to a sexual interrogation.

'Belinda, stop, stop, I'm serious, listen to me, and listen good, I've only got a few minutes left here, before the good Dr. misses me.'

Helga passed on her information; An American citizen of Dutch extract, she'd moved back to Holland five years ago with a primary mission of protecting American Corporations from Russian industrial espionage activities. She'd been working for the FBI Amsterdam offices all that time and her deep cover was her day job with Dr. Robbins.

'I'm sorry Belinda, I didn't want to get you involved, but I found some information concerning Steeles Pots and Pans. You're the only one I trust…. you've all been compromised; the blueprints and manufacturing plans for your new range of Trioxy Brillo products are under threat. There is a mole in your company, I'm so sorry but that's all I know….'

Belinda Blinked;

A mole in Steeles Pots and Pans… what was she to do? Who onever in this world could it be?

Giselle…?… Impossible,

Bella…?

Jim Thompson…?… not in a month of Tuesdays.

One thing was for certain, Steele's Pots and Pans was not going to fall on her watch…

Chapter 4

Belinda strutted into the central London Ritz cocktail bar all braless tits and swing. She marched up to a waiter and whispered;

'I am Belinda Blumenthal of Steele's Pots and Pans and I'm here for a top secret meeting with the one, the only, the incredibly sexy Duchess of Epsom.'

The waiter looked at her with some discomfort,

'No speekee Englash madmam.'

Belinda grimaced.

'Can I speak with your Manager please?'

The poor waiter gestured across the restaurant to his Boss who was seating people at their table and said,

'One minutes pliss.'

It was actually about seven and a half minutes before the restaurant Manager returned. It seemed the couple were being difficult if not downright demanding.

'My apologies madam for keeping you waiting, but the Duchess of Epsom is quite particular.'

He looked up at Belinda for the first time and quickly did a retake.

Belinda Blinked;

'Sam…. the youngish man on reception at the Horse and Jockey… is it you?' Belinda gurgled.

'Belinda…. Blumenthal… horsey outfit with the stunning tits… can it be true?'

They both laughed and Sam kissed Belinda on both cheeks…. very professionally.

'How can I assist you madam?'

'You won't believe this but I'm actually here to see the Duchess. Alone.'

Sam escorted Belinda to the Duchess's table and there she waited to be spoken to.

'Belinda!' exclaimed the Duchess, quickly putting away her reading glasses and looking up, 'How thoroughly wonderful to see you. Have you met -'

Belinda gasped at the woman next to the Duchess. It was the Contessa Luccia Lorenzo, Aldo Fellini's partner at the charity fuck session she and Alfonse Stirbacker had attended a week or so ago in Brussels;

'Good to see you again chica.' The Contessa kissed Belinda sexily.

'You too.' burbled Belinda, immediately ditching her previous plan.

'Come, sit, eat. They have a phenomenal reputation for their garlic smeared steak!'

The evening flew by and truth be told Belinda was glad of the distraction from her newish company worries.

'Right. It's time for a ladies night out!' the Duchess sparkled.

The steep dark steps down into the underground tavern that was known as Buckley's was not the best place for high heels and Belinda had her hands full keeping Luccia and The Duchess on their feet. Buckley's was rough, brash, sassy and down to earth with Motown music blaring throughout the old brick vaults. It was the sort of place to meet a bloke and get down to the sex. The Duchess whipped out her cheque book and paid the tab in advance, before slinking off on the arm of a muscle boy body builder with a tiny pea-head.

'Meet back here at One... right here!' she iterated over her left shoulder.

'Aren't you joining us, My Lady?' Belinda stupidly asked.

'No, I don't feel like Zachariah's magic wand tonight.'

The two ladies were shocked as they were firmly escorted through a fake boulder wall, then a curtain and into what could only be described as a middle eastern palace. Belinda was half annoyed at such a sudden change in scene, as she had been very much enjoying Martha Reeves and the Vandellas.

Nevertheless, Belinda and Luccia reclined on the sumptuous collection of puffy cushions, hassocks and carpet. Some had exquisite gold trim, some did not. Some had beautifully embroidered designs, some were plain. Some were made of velvet, some were made of hessian.

'I wonder who their middle-eastern supplier is?' Belinda thought. 'They could no doubt

use a quality cookware specialist to help with all their cooking.'

Just then, Zachariah strode into the secret drinking arena, small pyrotechnics exploded with a "pouf!" and from under the cushions carbon monoxide vapours slowly rose to the ceiling. The flamboyant night club owner bowed and sat next to the Contessa.

'Good evening my creatures of the puff!'

Zachariah cackled as he retrieved a long, thin cigar from the huge sleeves of his scintillating robes.

'I trust you know what this is?'

The women shook their heads, enraptured.

'Why it is the Tamarix flute!'

Belinda Blinked;

It could not be so. Belinda had heard the myths, but she wasn't dumb. A potent, yet totally safe, drug intoxication that stimulated in ways even the imagination could not envisage it. Indeed, this very famous cigar was so rare it was rumoured not to exist at all.

'Now, madam, you simply must spread your legs for me.'

Zachariah had dragged Belinda's mind back to the here and now. Without hesitation, she whipped off her thong and pulled her labial lids in two. Zachariah lay on his torso and lit a ruby red match. The flame was as green as Patrick O'Hamlin's homeland and made Belinda's innards look a little off in its light. Theatrically, Zachariah lit the mystic cigar and slowly placed it into his saliva creamed mouth. He breathed in deeply thoroughly enjoying the smoky goodness. Belinda shivered with excitement as he slid his mouth to her lids and filled her pussy with the hypnotic fumes.

Taking all ten of his fingers, Zachariah crimped her labia shut so she could feel the magical smoke marinade inside her. Well, it was really something and Belinda's senses could feel it all... but she'd be buggered if she had to describe it at a later date. When Zachariah finally let go, Belinda twitched and jiggled on the spot, in utter and complete utopia. Contessa Luccia was never one to be left out and she quickly turned 180 degrees pushing her perfect rear end into the sky. Zachariah didn't need telling twice and inhaled the cigar like a cavalry trooper. Sensually he pushed a long drag of smoke into her bottom hole. Clamping her ass shut for a couple of minutes, the Contessa too quickly began to get delirious as well.

'Ga Ga Goo' she moaned in her thick accent.

Belinda knew exactly what she meant. Suddenly there was no need for those expensive Italian language classes, she chuckled internally. However she was no time waster and she hopped onto her bent legs, scuttling like a hermit crab over to her newest best friend. Belinda's decapodic movement was successful in pushing herself into the royal's tush. Luccia opened up her bottom hole and allowed the zesty smoke to spiral into Belinda's vagina. The secondary sensation was so psychedelic that Belinda struggled to keep squatting over the Countessa's rump. Her legs were buckling, her clit was quivering as she was lost in the old mountain songs of Persia. Belinda collapsed onto the Turkish cushions and multi-coloured carpets a spent force.

Contessa Luccia instantly pounced on top of her and they kissed and kissed. It was at this precise second that Zachariah twirled on the spot three, maybe three and a half, times. When he came to a stand still, he was stark, ball-bag naked. He hungrily joined the women and they got down and messy with each other's sexual accoutrements. Three different people, three different cultures, equalled one jolly, marvellous, good time. And they fucked till the cows came home.

Chapter 5;

Turkey Sandwich?

Belinda and Luccia got redressed as best they could. The two girls pushed their way through the fake boulder wall to the bar and ordered a couple of Desperados. Zachariah had long disappeared into the seething mass of clubbers looking out for new challenges.

'Wow Belinda,' yelled Luccia over the groove tunes, 'that was a bit of rough all right!'

'You're telling me. And I don't smoke.'

They swigged back the cooling drinks and waited for the Duchess to rejoin them at the allotted hour. Bang on one-0-two-o'clock the Duchess joined them looking somewhat weather beaten. She'd lost her heels on the dance floor and she looked like she'd been pulled through a tree backwards.

'Belinda, girls...' she stuttered, 'I've had a fantastic time with two young men, but I'm shattered... can we go back to the hotel?'

'Just one problem ladies,' said the Contessa wearily, 'this is one hell of a bad place to get a taxi at this time of night.'

They all swore and Belinda said,

'I'm also going a different way to you two and that means two taxis!'

'Oh noooooooo!' chorused the aristocrats.

'You simply must stay in my suite.' said the Duchess, more to Belinda's ass than her head.

'Yes my lady.' Breathed Belinda as she pulled out her iphone and tapped in a string of numbers.

'Five minutes?... are you sure, OK we'll be outside. Ta!'

Outside the club it was cold and the girls huddled together. Suddenly a swish fluorescent orange Town Car pulled up to the kerb. Des Martin jumped out of the driver's seat and opened the rear doors for the girls.

'Great timing Des... as always!'

Des chuckled, doffed his chauffeur's hat and shut the doors.

'Where to ladies?' he asked while gunning the powerful engine.

'WHY THE RITZ OF COURSE!' the trio squawked in their poshest undertones.

The journey only took twenty three minutes to the hotel and Belinda invited Des in for a night cap.

'Sorry Boss, I've taped Match of the Day so need to get back to my bedsit, but I'll be seeing you!'

He tapped the peak of his cap and drove into the traffic. The Duchess was dead beat. She immediately excused herself, but promised to meet for breakfast before she went to her race meeting at Royal Windsor.

Luccia was the next to bail and the result was Belinda reclining back in her richly embroidered leather armchair with a bumper gin and slimlime tonic in her fist. Five minutes passed when suddenly a large voice coughed in her ear.

'Fancy a sandwich before some shuteye?' said Sam the Youngish Manager.

Deep in the vaults of the Ritz kitchens Sam carved Belinda yet another slice of turkey breast. He slapped it over her face and tantalisingly dropped it into her open mouth. She chomped on the divine meat in ecstasy. Sam stuffed some into his own mouth, took a long sharp knife and put it down. He kissed Belinda's lips.

Well fed, Belinda purred and leaned back on the stainless steel and spotless food preparation area. Sam removed her heels and kissed her bare fuchsia toenails with studs of stick on diamonds. Belinda shuddered with expectancy, she wiggled her ass and Sam picked up the hint on cue. With a gentle pull he removed her dress and threw it onto the fruit and vegetable rack. Belinda's thong quickly followed.

The Youngish Manager was all fingers and thumbs in her boggy pussy. Except for his left handed thumb which he'd burned earlier that day. Belinda was giddy with de ja vu as his indexes tapped and rapped at her spongy pubic typewriter. The very same fingers that had so expertly prepared those delicious turkey sandwiches were now releasing their expertise on a very accepting international sales director. And it wasn't long before her pussy started to sizzle.

Belinda was well thrilled. Knowing he was excited she cranked her head up to his twitching cock and glistened her puffy lips with his boyish sap.

'Such sweet syrup of the Norse Gods' she mused.

Just then the noises fell out of her head because Sam slid his throbbing cock into her vagina without so much as a by your leave. Belinda moaned and hoped the youngish Sam liked garlic and cigar smoke with his women. After a couple of very satisfactory moments Sam removed Belinda's brassiere. Sam held her tits in his hands. It did feel odd to be back in the promised land; her nipples were working overtime and their ripe shape had made him feel even more randy. He increased his stroke and

Belinda's hands tightened their hold onto the edge of the shiny stainless steel work area. She wanted to give Sam his full penetration and wondered how long it would take him to give her another massive orgasm. Her brain was reeling just thinking about it, she had to calm down, she had to concentrate. Belinda's juices started to pool on the stainless steel, Sam pulled out gently and said,

'Let's try this; I've always wanted to do this with you Belinda. The pro's call it, stand and carry.'

Sam pulled Belinda upright and held her tightly in his arms.

'Now wrap your legs around the top of my ass, tightly... you don't want to slip...'

Belinda willingly did as she was told, Sam was becoming a bit of a stud.

"Ccorrrrrr" she thought devilishly, 'what next?'

Sam's cock slid effortlessly into Belinda's hole in one. Once they were locked together Sam lifted Belinda off the stainless steel food preparation counter. He stepped back and swivelled Belinda round,

'Now, what shall we have a peek at?'

Sam started walking down the kitchen all the time penetrating Belinda who with the rhythm of the walking and Sam's thrusting was becoming more delirious with every second.

'Sam, Sam,' she groaned, 'keep going, don't stop, this is fucking marvellous...wait... is that more turkey over there?'

Belinda had spotted the original bird Sam had carved when they entered the kitchens.

'Why yes Belinda,' said an astonished Sam... 'Would you like a piece?'

'Yeesss... I love turkey... I love my friends... I love my job... I love Chardonnay!

The Youngish Manager Blinked;

Chapter 6;

Pots, Pans and Spoons;

It was 4.09 when Belinda's Jag pulled into the Steele's Pots and Pans carpark. She grabbed her brief case but left her overnight bag full of slinky negligés, kimonos and bloomers in the car. She'd brought it as a precaution as there was no telling how long this particular meeting would take.

Tony was waiting at the front doors looking harassed.

'This better be good Blumenthal. I've cut my honeymoon short for this.'

'It is sir,' replied Belinda, 'thanks to me and my network of associates we've been given advance warning on what could be a major disaster for this very company we call home.'

They walked down the corridor past Maeve on reception who smiled suspiciously at the business like faces of Belinda and her boss.

'Good afternoon Sir, Mrs Blumenthal. Can I help with anything?'

'No.' snapped Tony as they turned into the Leather Room.

As the doors closed behind them, Tony took a pair of black leather gloves off the hook at the back of the room. How odd. Belinda had never noticed them before. He proceeded to put them on and stroke the leather clad walls mystically. Leather on leather was a form of key and all of a sudden the large hide cubes started to shift and move. Just like a magic jigsaw puzzle, the walls began to reveal a long corridor of light with good, solid chrome doors at the end.

The hydraulic doors swooshed open and at the end of a space-age, long table sat Sir James Godwin's mighty body.

'Sit!' said Sir James gruffly, 'Speak!'

It only took Belinda ten minutes to tell all to her bosses. At the end of the brief presentation Tony had turned cream and Sir James buried his head in his hands and wept.

'I believe you Belinda, and your FBI source Helga. It all actually fits some amazing advances our development team at the factory, especially Professor Slinz, have been working on. We call it the Tri-oxy Brillo range and to be honest, it's a world beater.'

Tony whistled through his teeth, 'This could be worth millions to the company.'

'Billions,' echoed Sir James, 'it's a revolutionary metal design developed by Slinz. That and our recent uplift in sales will make us number one worldwide.'

'And that's the reason someone wants to steal the blueprints,' added Belinda, 'they want to make the money rather than us.'

Sir James set up his old fashioned flip chart which had never failed him. He handed the magic marker pen to Belinda and said,

'Let's brainstorm!'

'Sir James, I met Jim Walters from Apollo Security Agencies at the Epsom pile. He's ex-MI6 and still has good contacts, especially in the industrial espionage department. Is he worth retaining to help us with this problem?'

Sir James pondered the request for a second or so and said,

'Hmmm, yes, let's get some security on Professor Slinz, he's the key man in this project and if they kidnapped him, it would be the same as stealing the blueprints. I'll ring him now and get this all in motion. You two continue the brainstorm and let's see what you can dig up.'

Sir James left the room. Tony looked quizzically at Belinda and said,

'God Belinda, I don't know who the real spies are, you or our competitors.'

He laughed and took the marker pen from her.

'Now, who are our most ferocious competitors in the market place, whose nose have we put out of joint the most since you've arrived at our little company?'

'Ha!' Belinda replied, 'that's an easy one, it's the Germans, Bisch Herstellung from Berlin, they hate us!'

Tony wrote down the word Bisch on the flip chart.

'Any others?'

'Possibly Monroe Corp from the States after Bella's Jim Stirling deal and of course the Japanese conglomerate Hido Sakie. But overall I would go for Bisch.'

Tony wrote the other two names up and studied them for a while. He then wrote the nationality of the company under it. He immediately put a line through Monroe of the USA and wrote under it, FBI/CIA and Helga. He then did the same with Hido Sakie and wrote under it, small sales presence in Europe. Tony studied the Bisch column well, with Germany written under it and added Berlin. Then East Berlin. Belinda took the pen from him and added Amsterdam and Helga. She then ringed the words Berlin and Amsterdam and added FBI Europe; she then calmly drew a straight line between them.

'Bingo!' said Tony.

Belinda Blinked;

Seconds later Sir James returned beaming and pointed at Belinda.

'You Belinda, have a meeting at the Pentra at 9.00pm tonight with Jim Walter's MI6 contact. He'll make contact with you at the long bar... where you and the Glee Team drink...'

Belinda moved to leave the top secret, modern meeting room.

'But remember there is a mole loose in this organisation. Utter of this to no one. Not even the kindly ladies or valued spouses of Steele's Pots and Pans.'

Tony's face fell to the mirrored desk.

'The three of us are as wide as this gets. Hrrmmph, now get going now, and Belinda, thanks!'

Belinda smiled at Sir James' gratitude and left immediately for London.

The Pentra long bar was busy as Belinda ordered her first Gin and Tonic of the day from Paddy the bartender. She relaxed back into her bar stool and looked around for men lounging against doorways in long trench coats, quietly tapping their ears as they communicated with their handlers... but she couldn't identify any. Half an hour passed but nothing happened, she ordered another Gin and Tonic. Paddy thought she'd been stood up and wished he was off duty.

'Drinking on the job Ms. Blumenthal? Would Sir James approve?'

Belinda looked to her left; one of a group of salesmen had detached himself from the edge of his party and was talking to her.

'Leave me alone chump. I've got a man to meet' Belinda barked.

'The very same, do you mind if I join you?'

Belinda took a minute and looked him up and down. Decent well-polished shoes, goodish physique, a full head of dark hair and a to die for smile.

'The name's Spooner. James Spooner.'

'Oh fuck the Norse gods all at once'. Belinda shrieked. 'You're the man I've been waiting for!'

They spent the next two hours getting to know each other, and then it was suddenly time to call it a night. Spooner walked Belinda to her suite door and kissed her deeply on the crown of her head as he said goodnight. Belinda felt her vagina moisten, it was never wrong, she wanted this spy to investigate her insides. A thorough exploration was required, leaving no crease unturned. She stroked the contours of his partially shaven cheek and with her other hand felt for his cock. It was aroused, perfect she thought, she calmly unzipped him as he held her against her room door.

Spooner took a step backwards to the opposite side of the corridor. He twisted his left cufflink 90 degrees and aimed it right at her. A razor thin red laser beam pierced her forehead.

'Oh no... what's happening,' wept Belinda's brain, 'what if this was not who he seemed?'

Spooner slowly moved the cufflink downwards and with it the laser beam travelled past Belinda's eyelashes, over her upturned nose, down her puffy lips and past her chin. Terrified, she began to smell smoke and she looked downward dreading the worst. Sure enough the laser was burning her cocktail dress right down the middle. Past her breasts, over her belly button, all the way to her knees. It had even burned through her brazier and favourite glitter thong.

Suddenly her dress, her undergarments and her womanly secrets fell to the ground either side of her naked body. Her eyes moved upwards and gazed into her opposite number.

Spooner winked with a devilish charm.

Belinda Blinked;

Chapter 7;

Copier blues;

Spooner;

James Spooner and Belinda Blumenthal breakfasted together as the lovers they had portrayed the previous evening in the corridor outside Belinda's room. It was obvious to any casual or not so casual onlooker that they were having an affair and that suited Spooner down to the ground.

As he tucked into his full English with all the trimmings, including tomatoes, mushrooms, bacon, Cumberland sausage, beans, black pudding and granary toast (white would not be healthy enough for a member of Her Majesty's spy network) he thought about last night. His mind pictured Belinda on the sumptuous one inch long, tea-stained bed runner. Completely naked and on all fours, she had her tits hanging down waiting for him to fuck her deliciously wide open, closely shaven, vagina from behind. He loved it, a worthy last shag on earth if Steele's Pots and Pans were to be his downfall.

Belinda could hardly eat. Her head was racing with thinking about Bisch.

'Why do these things always happen to me?' whined Belinda. 'Why can't I just be left alone to sell some pots and pans!'

The plan was simple; Spooner was to be the latest temporary recruit to the Steele's Pots and Pans team. He would be working as an IT freelancer under Belinda's supervision giving him a free hand to visit both the factory in Scotland and head office in London. Only Tony, Sir James and Belinda knew of his true role and it was imperative that it stayed that way. In the best of circumstances it was always hard to catch a mole, but a recently established one was the worst. Spooner knew from bitter experience that they just didn't make mistakes. That only came later in their careers when they became lazy or reckless.

Later that day Belinda was introducing her very own mole around Steele's HQ with a haughtiness born from the knowledge of secrets unbeknown to her colleagues. And so it was, Spooner met all and sundry from Jim Thompson to Gladys the canteen dinner lady, who got a much savoured peck on her wrinkled cheek. Bella rose on her teetering stilettos as Belinda ushered James Spooner into her office. She put her gooseberry yoghurt with papaya slivers she was eating down in a hurry. The slimy snack unfortunately slopped over onto her keyboard. It definitely didn't look professional... and Bella did so want to look professional in front of Belinda and her new guest.

'James Spooner, meet our International Sales Key Account Manager who likes eating yoghurt off her keyboard, Bella Ridley.'

'Pleased to meet you Bella, just call me Spoons!'

Belinda laughed as the flustered Bella shook his hand.

Belinda went back to her office and picked up her phone. She quickly dialled James Spooner's desk phone. He picked up his phone.

'Spoons, I'm going to have Bella and Giselle out of the office this afternoon so you can search their desks and stuff. When you've done what you have to, get Jim Thompson to drive you over to the Pentra. You can then start to assess them both when they've had a few drinks down them. Ciao!'

Spooner grunted, put the phone down and started to assess Bella's delicious ass as she bent over the copy machine which had just jammed on her.

'Can I help you… Bella?' he crooned.

'Why Spoons,' said Bella breathlessly, 'that would be just wonderful.' as she unbuttoned a button on her button-down silk blouse.

'You don't want ink to splash all over you.'

'No, no I don't Mr. IT man. And you should know!'

Bella removed her bra, unbuttoned her mini-skirt and stepped out of her thong. Spooner set to work investigating her from her toenails to her scrunchie.

'Then what happened?' gushed Belinda.

Two thirds of the famous Glee Team were drinking the best Chilean chardonnay in the Pentra Long bar, tittle-tattling as only they knew how.

'Well I'm sorry to tell you he didn't get as far as fucking me.' said Bella. 'I wasn't devastated, but I felt let down…. hungry is probably a better word.'

Belinda nodded and felt strangely upset on Bella's behalf.

Bella continued, 'Whilst dressing me he asked a few questions about my visiting Europe, especially Germany. Of course I quickly filled him in on Jim Stirling and Hank Skank and how they were my key customer. To be honest, he sort of lost interest in me. I even had to button up my own blouse… really strange Belinda… perhaps he's well… different?'

Belinda nodded sagely and said. 'I think you've hit the nail on the head Bella, he is different, but so like us… do you reckon he's bi?

Bella knocked back her Chardonnay and nodded at Paddy for a refill.

'Belinda if he is bi, I'd love to see him … we could be in for one hell of a great six months while he's with the company.'

Belinda laughed out loud for the first time that day.

'Well if he is bi I'd love to see him handle Jim Thompson.'

A hidden stress had been lifted from her; Spooner had obviously cleared Bella from being the mole by his subtle questioning of her travel details. Suddenly life was good again!

Back in the office's James Spooner reflected on his very satisfactory interview of International Key Account Manager Bella Ridley. She did indeed have a beautiful ass, never mind her stunning tits, but best of all there was no way in his professional opinion she was the mole. On reflection however, he'd been wrong before and would no doubt be wrong again, but for the moment at least, Ms. Ridley was in the clear.

His mind turned to Blumenthal; she wouldn't be the first mole to create a diversion which then quickly diverted suspicion away from her own activities. He knew she was out this afternoon, so he got up and walked along the corridor to Belinda's office.

Spooner picked the lock with his trusty knitting needle and let himself in. He sat down on the big black faux leather swivel chair which Belinda loved so much and flicked open her Filofax. The week came into view... Paris.... Penelope Pollet... didn't sound dangerous.

Saturday week came into view, 10.45am City Airport; flight to Scotland; Factory visit with the Glee Team; Return Sunday pm.

Spooner's hackles rose on the back of his neck, Blumenthal hadn't informed him of her little visit to Scotland, this was indeed a turn up for the books. Was she making contact with her handler? Here at last was a good solid line of enquiry, he'd take the last flight out next Friday night and set up a little surveillance op.

'Excuse me, should you be in here?'

Spooner immediately swiveled Belinda's big black chair to face the door. A stunningly beautiful girl with a bit of a blonde crazy hairdo was facing him.

Spooner Blinked;

Chapter 8

Cricklewood Pumping Station;

'I'm terribly sorry Miss, I'm new. Ms. Blumenthal has been complaining about her computer being slow.'

Giselle smiled, 'Of course... I'm not surprised, typical... just like her lovers... aahhhh... I remember, James Spooner.... IT specialist isn't it? A six month contract if I remember rightly?'

'Yes, computers and all that rubbish.... you see, many professionals opt to keep their PC machines running for months on end, never physically shutting it down. I believe this is the case here. Thus I'm going to give this here computer a little break. Now, I can either delete some programs Ms. Blumenthal isn't using or I can shut her down for a couple of seconds to minutes.... now if this doesn't work then it could be infected with a spot of malware. That doesn't have such a simple solution and would need to be looked at in more detail.'

Giselle delicately blushed; she hadn't quite expected the hunk that James Spooner was. A spindly, weedy type of IT nerd was somehow more acceptable.

'I'm Mrs Sylvester... you can call me Giselle, you know, the Managing Director's PA and wife.'

Spooner got up and gently shook Giselle's hand.

'I'm actually here to drive you to the Pentra for your meeting with the Glee Team. Meet you in reception in 5.'

Spooner nodded his understanding, got up and left the room with his heart beating rather more rapidly than he'd liked. This Giselle creature was definitely his sort of thing, after all, Belinda and Bella were quite robust sort of creatures, but this Giselle, she was sort of a racehorse against a pair of mules.

Spooner's clinical mind clicked into operational mode, espionage music started playing in his head as he bounded down the staircase to reception... no lifts for him he was on the case and his next interview was going to be... well let's put it this way.... very interesting.

Back in her office Giselle removed her wedding ring from her finger and dropped it into her pencil tray. Her drive to the Pentra was going to be the long way round and would include passing a few reservoirs she knew.

However, before even starting the Jaguar, Giselle had managed to lean over and instruct the very willing James as to where to insert his seatbelt. She let her breast tits touch his waist and leg as she did so, and made sure to brush his cock with her left wrist.

It wasn't long before they had reached a secluded spot on the banks of Brent reservoir. Giselle parked the car and looked at Spooner.

'Good day for ducks. Fancy a swim?'

Spooner's eyes lit up. He knew this code alright. He knew he wanted this woman, she was hot and the hotter he could make her, then the better she'd fuck.... and the more innocent her answers would be to his subtle questioning technique.

The duo fumbled their clothes off and ran into the fresh water supply hand in hand like the protagonists in some romantic novella. Spoons let his cock assume it's true position whist his dark haired chest winked at Giselle.

'Please me Spooner, oh please, please me!'

He entered her along with a good amount of water, in and out and out and in he went.

Giselle started to intermittently gently scream as they writhed in the reservoir.

Suddenly a loud voice from the left bank interrupted the investigation.

'Oi get out of there! That's our drinking water you wretched pair of rats and you're spoilin me fishin!'

The trashing couple looked up and saw an oldish fly fisherman in green wellies up to his waist. But Spooner couldn't care a fuck and started to shag Giselle with greater zest.

'Get out! OUT OUT OUT!' The fisherman started to wade into the reservoir reeling back his rod.

Giselle and Spooner waded out of the water. They ran through the reeds and skipped over the barbed wire fence into an old, deserted Victorianesque but beautiful building of architectural integrity. They ran up the spiral staircase that led all the way to the top of the statuesque chimney and there they waited.

Spooner unlatched his leather ankle bracelet of charms and connected the top bit to the bottom bit and then to the middle bit. After a few minutes of assembly there was a perfectly formed pair of miniature binoculars.

'How nifty' Giselle mused. 'Old Spoons must be a boy scout.'

Spooner looked out of the tower. He could see the oldish fisherman beating the reeds with his fishing rod, obviously in search of the nudist spoilers.

'We should probably wait a few wee moments for him to beat himself tired, dearest Giselle.'

'Works for me.' proclaimed the MD's new wife as she opened her legs wide and stuffed his face into her half open muff. There Spoons slurped and Giselle gagged for air. Her sopping wet clitoris had rarely been entertained so handsomely. Her delirious mind had become mush with the massive adrenaline rush. Spooner's tongue had proven better than many of the cocks she'd entertained in the past... not least her husband's.

She pushed Spoons's head out of herself and he wiped his face with a wet wipe again pulled from his leg ankle bracelet. He studied the still twitching Giselle. Time to pump this one for information in the grand pumping station of Cricklewood on Thames he sumarised.

'Do you get home much Giselle, I mean, you can't have learnt to enjoy my technique without some initial training... Belgian I'd say.'

'James,' Giselle panted, 'I could say the same for you, but yes my mother is Flemish and in truth she's spent time in Belgium and Holland.'

'Ahh, that explains it then,' replied Spooner, 'let me expand, your words and voice change as you experience your deepest release, I'm pretty certain you were speaking Flemish at the height of your orgasm.'

'And what orgasm was that James...?'

Spooner was taken aback. Spoons Jr hadn't let him down... well not since boarding school and the lights out incident with prefect Tommy Stoneshire in Devonshire Wing.

Giselle goggled at his eyes and ran her ten fingers through her hair. With a manic laugh she threw the tufts of hair that had been caught in her knuckles into the air!

'I did orgasm! Haha oh did I cum! And I'm hungry for more. Come dip your ladle into my punch bowl, Mr Spooner!'

She pounced on him and started kissing him everywhere. Just as his cock was resurrected she threw him over so that he was on his front and started to lick his hairy bottom. No more words were uttered.

Just jolly old sex….

Chuuuuuuurrrrrrrrrr. Chuuuuuuurrrrrrrr.

'Hmmmmmm. A bit more.'

Chuuuuuuurrrrrrrrrr. Chuuuuuuurrrrrrrr. Shurr.

'That's it!' she exclaimed.

Belinda adjusted her webcam slightly so she could see herself fully on the screen. She nodded, admiring her glorious, full bush. She had decided to grow it out as a fashion accessory to her Parisian business trip. She was with clippers in hand, well blissful.

But then her office was invaded with people.

Oh Brother! Belinda had forgotten all about the bi-daily strategy meeting with the RSMs.

'Come in lads' she said, brushing some pubes off her desk and pulling up pants.

She did so enjoy addressing the troops, in fact she now saw herself as one of the greatest bosses in British kitchenware and never forgot her white-collar motto;

"Life was great when you got what you wanted… and helped others to do the same."

'Patrick O'Hamlin, Regional Sales Manager for Scotland and Ireland; Speak.'

Patrick O'Hamlin rose to his cockles nervously.

'We have a slight issue with Mullet supermarkets, boss.'

'But they're one of our biggest regionals, what have you not done, you stupid goon?'

'Nothin… Miss.'

'Don't sell me a dog Patrick O'Hamlin. I demand to know the truth!'

'Well, their account is 30 days standard terms; they want 60 days standard terms to put us into prime spot. It would be worth it, but Credit Control aka Trevor fucking Ditherhead has knocked them on the nose… not once, but twice.'

'And I presume the opposition are prepared to do this to take the business?' Belinda pondered aloud.

Patrick sighed, 'Yes and what's worse it's those Germans at Bisch.'

Belinda's body hairs all jumped up at once setting her teeth at edge.

'Leave it with me.' she spoke.

'Ken Dewsbury, Regional Sales Manager for Central and North England; Speak.'

'I'm a bit buggered boss. I mislaid a shipment of couscous evaporators. So I'm down 643%.'

'And you were last month's top seller, eh? Well a lesson there for everyone curtesy of Ken fucking Dewsbury: one day you're cock of the walk, the next a feather duster.'

Ken shifted his moist eyes to the floor.

'Des Martin, Regional Sales Manager for London and the Home Counties. Speak.'

'South East and London sales figures are up by 217% boss.'

'Ahhh, that is a happy cabbage, Des. You get 5 minutes…. see me afterwards…. or now even.'

'Yes Sir… Boss!' Des Martin punched the air. Belinda unbuttoned her blouse and pulled out one of her tits. Des smouched his way up onto her lap and started to suck, slurp and nibble her nipple like the pro he was.

'Now, any more business?' Belinda continued.

'I'm just confirming the exact timing of your Fivecarre Hypermarkets meeting this evening.' said Jim Thompson.

'Fab dabby doosie Jim.' smiled Belinda. 'Busy, busy, busy;'

The Paris taxi struggled through the evening traffic. Tonight was her opportunity to bring on board one of the biggest retailers the world knew. Penelope Pollet was no slouch and Belinda knew all too well that new contacts were the blood of life for any sales girl.

Belinda was ready to trade; a simple long black dress with matching heels, purse and a sparkling necklace was all she needed.

She made her way through the opulent bar; ordered a cocktail and waited for Penelope to arrive. A sudden lull in the bar conversation of 'Oh la las' heralded the arrival of an exquisitely dressed French lady. She was wearing a daringly tailored pink linen suit with orange seaming.

Belinda immediately recognised her to be Penelope Pollet, world-wide head of purchasing for Fivecarre Hypermarkets.

They kissed in French fashion and Belinda ordered a French Martini for Penelope. They sat at the bar and chatted about horses, jumping and the steady progress of Penelope's daughter.

'Now Belinda, I need just five minutes of your ear before the show to talk about our business opportunity.' said Penelope.

'Show??!' stammered Belinda. 'Oh please tell me we are catching a play at the Moulin Rouge! I've always longed to go and watch the knickerless dancing whores.' she gushed.

Penelope Pollet spat some of her very French Martini into her glass.

'Non non non, you simple bitch, it iz all about La Moulin Marron.'

'The Brown Windmill?' gawped Belinda's perfect translation. Yes it was true she'd never heard of it.

'Now, ze quality of ze oxybrillo iz good; Jim Thompzon iz ze darling and my people vant to work with him. But... can you help us with store merchandising as you have absolutely no past record with us. What I mean iz marketing support; you pay us to get your pans in ze hands of ze housewife.'

'Penelope, it's so refreshing to meet someone who asks for what they want and why! Of course we can assist. I can authorise 10% support here and now, have we a deal?'

'Ha ha, I can zee the perfect close that you are offering me, OK, it iz good enough to start our relationship, but we vill keep negotiating, OK?'

Belinda downed her cocktail in one.

The newly minted business associates and blossoming best friends took their seats in the privatised Fivecarre corporate box of La Moulin Marron and watched the show.

The long legged dancing girls were as stunning as at the neighbouring establishment beginning with the French word for 'red' and the years old choreography was timeless perfection.

'You know Belinda, you can call me P-P, Penelope iz a bit formal and right now it iz what I truly am... Penelope Pizzed, hic!'

All of a sudden every light, candle and mobile phone went out in the Moulin Marron. It was as black as the skin of an aubergine and no one could see a thing. Then a spotlight as hot as the dancing girls swooshed upwards.

From the roof a huge ball made up of a thousand and one balloons tied together with liquorice shoelaces was lowered downwards. The audience was silent wondering what it could all mean... just as they were wondering what it all meant, a chubby arm stuck itself out from the bunch of balloons. It was holding a very massive and pointy carrot. The meaty arm quickly popped one of the balloons with the carrot and in doing so revealed a bit of wobbly flesh to the whole Moulin Marron.

The audience applauded and just as they did so, the arm popped another balloon, revealing a hunk of thick thigh. Little bite sized pieces of ham, cheese and baguette rained down on the congregation.

'A little midnight cruditee for the hungry mob.' spoke Penelope with the knowledge.

As more balloons were burst, more bits and bobs of food showered the watching men and lady more two who soon guzzled their finger food, all the while whooping at the insane striptease above them.

Eventually the last balloon was popped and the most plump roly-poly babe was revealed in all her glory. She was so big she indeed resembled a balloon herself thought Belinda a bit meanly. But, she didn't mean it to be mean.

No. In fact Belinda had not blinked for the duration of the performance. She was transfixed, mesmerized, awake.

'P-P, who the fuck is that yummy, scrummy wrecking ball of a woman?'

'Why, she iz ze one, ze only Mistress Sweetjuice. And she haz requested a private audience wiz you...'

Belinda Blinked;

P-P led Belinda up the winding staircase into the all seeing eye of the Moulin Marron. The circular room was a sumptuous chocolate box of interior design. Everything was a different shade of brown.

'I do so hope you hav not eaten too recently, dearest Belinda, for Mistress Sweetjuice iz a world eminent feeder.' P-P cackled.

Belinda was intoxicated with buzz, she had heard of this kink but never thought herself lucky enough to indulge in it personally. Let alone in a windmill atop the city of lust. Somewhere distant a bugle sounded and all the lamps went out, then on again.

A sail of the windmill passed, it's eye revealing the rotund figure of Mistress Sweetjuice. She was head to toe in a skin tight, white latex bodysuit with a dog collar studded with liquorice all sorts. She even had a tail of flumps which she was swinging dominantly.

Belinda had never seen a sexier sight in all her years as a resident of planet earth.

'So thiz iz the famous pots and pans mademoiselle?'

'Yes, I am Belinda Blumenthal. It's an honour to meet you Mistress Sweetjuice.'

'SILENCE!' howled the Mistress as she cracked her marshmallow whip on Belinda's outstretched hand.

'Pardon... uhh pardon.' Belinda murmured.

'I hope you iz hungry cherie.' P-P said as she took her viewing stool on the edge of the circular room. Mistress Sweetjuice shook her lack mouth and gobbled like a chicken.

'Oh fuck me, take me, screw me but please don't tease me... I beg you, Mistress Sweetjuice.' pleaded Belinda a bit desperately to be honest with you.

'I want you undraped of these rags!' the Mistress shouted.

Belinda removed her whole dress in one, parading her shaggy pussy.

'Ah may Oui! OUIIIIII.' the Mistress grunted.

Because of her conversational level French Belinda knew she had made the correct grooming decision and basked in her deep knowledge of European culture preferences.

'Get in these heels.' said the Mistress as she threw a jazzy pair of eight inch platforms at her. '

Belinda strapped them in, ensuring the Velcro was secure.

'What now?' she asked.

'INSOLENCE!' screamed the Mistress as she whipped Belinda again.

God, each crack was turning her on more and more she swore....

'Lick me 'til I sparkle!'

'What?' Belinda questioned internally, 'how does that work?'

A chubby finger wriggled like a worm indicating her to come closer. Belinda teetered in the heels towards the Dominatrix. The closer she got, the better she could see. About three and a half paces away it became clear that Mistress Sweetjuice's suit wasn't latex at all. Two and a half paces away showed it was paint. One and a half paces away;

No!!! smoothed whipped cream!

Belinda sank to her knees and began eating the thin layer of room temperature cream off her bubbly body. Slowly she began to see Mistress Sweetjuice in all her majesty. It was a body the likes of which she was unfamiliar but ever so attracted to. Even dairy free, her huge nipples were barely visible on her whiter than white breasts.

Belinda slurped Mistress Sweetjuice's every curve and bodily opening with felicity. It took hours, but with the methodical mastery of a truffle hog, Belinda scrubbed the form until it was well polished.

'Success!' she panted as Mistress Sweetjuice beamed at her, clapping her flaps in applause.

'Now, tickle my clit and drink me dry!'

'YES MISTRESS SWEETJUICE!' Belinda squealed as she prepared to go below decks.

Mistress Sweetjuice spread her legs like Flora ProActiv over a soft brioche bun. The ease in which she did so impressed Belinda and so she set to work.

Belinda delicately started to lick Mistress Sweetjuice's vagina, trying to avoid the cream flecked pubes. My God her namesake was not wrong. Her oozing leakage tasted like a French summer in the Algarve. Another-worldly concoction of Burgundy and pongy cheese.

Sweetjuice opened her vaginal lids and Belinda was fully in. As perceptive as a red squirrel she found the clitoris. It didn't take long and the French clitoris was soon sopping wet and its owner was groaning in anticipation of the orgasm that was surely just around the bend.

As it was told, her screams could have woken the gargoyles of Notre Dame and Belinda surveyed the juddering mess of a woman on the antique lino with silver trim.

'God I'm good!' Belinda proudly proclaimed.

The next morning Belinda boarded the EuropaLine bullet train to London. Despite her churning stomach, she had been somewhat dreading her first trip to the Steele's Pots and Pans factory since she started her post all those months ago. She boarded the plane at City Airport and after a brief connection in Hull, turbocharged geographically upwards to Scotland.

Belinda enjoyed the shortbread cubes onboard and by the time she had landed at the McDonald Scotland Airport she was feeling much better physically. She was ready for some Celtic fun and nonsense with her favourite Glee Team pals, Giselle and Bella.

James Spooner watched Belinda Blumenthal from behind the cover of a Scottish 'Highlands and Islands' morning newspaper as she waited for a taxi outside the airport. It was surprisingly raining and Belinda hadn't brought her trench coat. James felt like going over to her and offering her his, but he knew he couldn't do that. The investigation had quickly escalated within Whitehall's corridors of power and the situation was now a purple-red alert.

Eventually the International Sales Director disappeared into the interior of a white taxi slightly bedraggled. As James watched the cab pull away he raised his hand and an unmarked car skidded to a halt at the kerb.

'Follow that taxi Mimi!' he shouted to the driver who was sporting a beautiful Bob style haircut. He hopped in and they speeded off. Keeping a safe distance, Mimi followed Belinda to where she was headed. The two spies watched prudently as she paid off her taxi bill. She was outside a large church. She cautiously looked around herself for wandering eyes before ringing the big old bell. After a moments pause Belinda was greeted by a mystery figure and quickly smuggled inside the stone.

James Spooner Blinked;

He had her in his sights and was under no circumstances going to let her out of his sight...

Chapter 11;

The meet…;

Belinda thanked the altar boy for letting her into the big room outside of opening hours. It was 100% empty. Except for a few balding monks, an organ cleaner thrushing it's pipes with a groan and a hum and an old crone praying in one of the pews.
Belinda swooshed across the flagstones and snuck in beside the hag. She waited patiently until the woman noticed her presence by the way of her potent Lavender de Liquefaction perfume. It didn't take long.

The coughing crone turned to Belinda and said 'What did the nightingale sing to the dustman?'

Belinda looked around herself before answering: 'Mr Bojangles'

The crone smiled a toothy smile. 'You made it then.'

'Yes just as you said. I am….'

Suddenly Belinda was cut off when the crone's tin of cough mints stared to beep. She flicked it open and brought the box to her ear, listening intently. She gasped and turned to face Belinda nose to nose.

'You've been compromised.' she croaked.

'Impossible?' spluttered Belinda. 'I changed at Hull.'

'Well they've followed you. An evil agent is on your toenails. We've gotta get out of here. Pronto.'

Chest pains of inadequacy pounded Belinda's heartstrings as she followed the crone down past the altar and backstage.

Just as they slipped out of sight James Spooner entered the church. He slinked across the marble like the spy he truly was, sensing the presence of a dissenting businesswoman and her accomplice.

He readied his gun and started to inspect behind each pillar, certain to expose his prey.
The moment he reached behind the altar was the exact minute Belinda and the crone bundled into their getaway car. And zip they were gone.

Thirty eight minutes later the two women were finally in the safety of Belinda's hotel suite. The crone turned to face Belinda and immediately started scratching at her face. Gradually the wrinkled skin flaked off revealing the warm features of Agent Helga.

'We are in grave danger Miss Blumenthal.' she gasped in her native Texas drawl.

'Yes I don't have a doubt about it whatsoever.' Belinda replied as she started to strip the FBI angel of her rags. It wasn't long before her tits were pounding in the sales woman's fists and her pussy was drooling.

Belinda shook off her wet clothes and kicked them into a corner. The women led one another to the slender coffee table and began to chow down.
They were sopping and screaming and dreaming and believing when the desktop telephone rang.
Helga stuffed her labia further into Belinda's mouth ensuring her silence. The agent dropped her own voice to a hushed whisper of a sound lost on the winds.

'It's probably bugged. Let me.'

Belinda nodded between her legs as Helga answered the old rotary phone in an accent.

''Lo. Maid.'

The seconds past as she listened to the person who had called the telephone.

Helga Blinked;

'It's the front desk.' she said. 'They say your fiancé is here.'

Belinda Blinked;

'He says he's meeting you here.' Helga felt cheated and bereft at the same time...

'What the fuck is going on Belinda? You've just been slobbering all over me... Ohh... I see it... you'll do anything to get me to tell you about your espionage case...'

'Don't be stupid Helga... what fiancé; I'm Belinda Blumenthal.... I don't do fiancées...'

'OK,' replied a sulky Helga, 'lie to me all you want, but he's downstairs; waitin...'

'Well send him up. I have nothing to hide.' said Belinda breezily as she spread her perfect legs enticing her American chum.

Helga huffily told reception to send up Belinda's future husband and the girls made themselves look presentable. Just as Helga was tucking her blouse into her slacks she stopped dead.

'Hang on. Suppose he's the bad spy guy from the church?'

'Oh fuuuuuuck' screamed Belinda, 'we surely have met our maker.'

'Crap' yelled Helga as she unobtrusively pulled her automatic pistol out from under the sofa cushion and held it ready in her right hand.

She clicked the safety catch just as the door knocked. She opened the door.

'Stand steady cowboy,' Helga hissed at the man, 'raise your arms, NOW!'

Belinda screamed.

'SPOONER???!'

Helga's heart fell. It truly was Belinda's fiancé.

'Now Fianceee,' drawled Helga in her southern Texan accent, 'drop your piece.'

Spooner looked at Belinda, who nodded and Spooner pulled his gun from his trousers waistband dropping it onto the ugly brown patterned carpet.

'Good boy,' breathed Helga, 'Belinda, pick it up and bring it to me.'

Belinda looked into Spooner's eyes and said,

'James, it's OK, she's FBI and with us, just do as she says and we'll all be able to move on quickly.'

Spooner nodded his head and somehow started to relax, if Belinda was the mole, he'd be dead by now.

'OK Mr Fianceee,' drawled Helga, 'let's remove your jacket and shirt.'

Spooner removed the light European issue leather coat and his 'breathable in any situation' Marks & Spencer shirt. He calmly threw them away as if it was something he did every time he was questioned by a romantically beautiful looking woman with a pistol pointing at his vitals.

'Now your shoes; socks...well everything' Spooner nodded his understanding that she wanted him naked, whilst Belinda giggled and thought,

'Helga is really pissed at his choice of cover story; he'll be dammed lucky if she doesn't fuck him.'

The perceptive Blumenthal was not far wrong and once James Spooner had corroborated all of Belinda's story Helga put her pistol down and stripped off. Belinda did too of course, there was no way she was letting Helga have this hunk of a man meat to herself that rainy Scottish evening.

The girls laid him down on the long table and squatted on either side of his face. Their vagina's rubbed his stubble, slowly working their way down his body.

'Draw your weapon Agent Spooner!' shouted Belinda and Spoon's cock immediately became erect.
Belinda fucked the two spies with virtuoso vigour as Spooner took his turn inside each of them. But he was an MI5 professional and he knew when he was about to climax so he reversed out of Belinda's tunnel of devotion and creamed himself into her bellybutton.

Belinda giddy with twitching aftershocks scooped the whiteish gunk out of her borehole and devoured it down the hatch. But just as she did the old phone rang again.

Bold as a brass monkey Belinda swallowed, grabbed it and listened. After a moment and a half she placed down the phone line.

'Who was it?' asked Spoons still panting and mopping his brow with his Y-fronts.

'It's the factory. Prof Slinz wants to meet the Glee team tomorrow. But what if the mole is there? I'm too scared to enter that building alone. What if I never come out?'
'No. You must go.' drawled Helga with typical American directness.

'But it must be where the blue prints for the new Tri-Oxy Brillo range are. It's too dangerous. I'm just a middle management senior sales executive...'

'She's right Belinda. You have to go;

For Queen;

For Country;

And for Steele's Pots and Pans.'

She looked aghast from male agent to female agent.

Belinda Blinked;

Chapter 12;

A Factory Visit;

James Spooner changed suits. He hated the smell of stale seamen, and no matter how careful one was you always felt that a few splashes would linger in a visible place. Helga had slipped away as was customary by critters of her vocation line.

Belinda was still sleeping despite it being 6:24 in the morning. But there was no time for more playfulness as it was the day of the factory visit.

Belinda walked into the large industrial doors with authority reflective of her rank. But her professionalism was burst like an over-pumped lilo the moment she saw her bosom gal pals, Giselle and Bella.

'Giselle and Bella! We're back together!' she shouted.

They all shrieked, formed a little circle and sang.

'G for Gin, T for tonic,

Our six titties are supersonic!

We don't mind men,

We don't like fuss.

We're the Glee Team...

Come and get us!'

They bumped bottoms and flew their hands in the air fluttering their fingers like falling raindrops. A miniature cough broke the joyousness and the women looked down at a smallish white coated, grey bearded gent.

'Gud mornink Frau Sylvester and Frauleins Ridley and Blumenthal. I am ze eminent Professor Slinz, inventor extraordinaire of Steele's Pots and Pans. Please follow me for your access, all areas, tour of our vonderful factory...'

A fluttering honey bee of an Irish lilt broke the forthright handedness.

'Please don't start without me.' it said. The Glee Team flicked their pony tails in unison as they swiveled to see little Maeve from Steele's reception desk totter towards them. What was SHE doing here Belinda thought.

It was all Bella could do to keep her tongue from polishing the tiles her mouth was so wide open in shook. Maeve barged past Bella, past Giselle and even past Belinda cocking an outstretched hand to the wizened clever clogs.

'You must be Professor Slinz' she said with determined plainness. Slinz viewed the newest arrival as the leaf of her homeland and so couldn't believe his luck. Four lovely ladies to show off to. It beat his previous life fashioning cauldrons on the streets of Hanover he thought.

'OK girlies now ve start!'

As they walked through the thick metal doors Belinda was fascinated by her surroundings. The largish laboratory was bursting with life and she could see pots and pans scattered all over various benches with technicians busily turning on jets of flame and burning out their centres. She had always admired factory workers and their specialist skill sets. But then she choked on her praise. There, in amongst the workforce and behind a blow torch was Agent Helga disguised as a welder.

Helga flashed Belinda an eye that said,

'Don't notice me, don't bother me...' and it was an eye Belinda immediately understood. This was what deep cover looked like and it was turning her on like a spin wash at 40 degrees.

'Now as you iz all empoyiz ov ze company I shall introduce you to ze top secret, untold vonder zat iz ze Tri Oxy Brillo Range.' he said.

The women were salivating as Slinz shuffled over to the life sized safe in the corner of the room. Slinz entered the combination and opened the door. Gold light flooded out from within as the women gawped in awe.

'Velcome to ze future of Potz and Panz!' the Professor proclaimed.

Brushing aside A2 sheets of graph paper containing the intricate blueprints, Professor Slinz selected a deep saucepan from the sparse collection of gold leaf prototypes.

The Glee Team and Maeve gasped in wonderment as he set it onto a metal table top. Next Professor Slinz took from the wall mounted spice rack a larger than a litre test tube full to the brim of the highest quality Scotland highland spring water.

'Votch' he said.

Prof Slinz took the test tube between his fore and ring fingers and poured the Scottish highland spring water into the pan. Upon making contact with the base it immediately started to bubble and boil.

'Von hundreds degreez like ziz' he laughed as he snapped his thumb and middle finger.

'Self heating pans in three secondz - I give you Ze Tri Oxy Brillo Range!'

After a few moments the Glee Team and Maeve burst into applause. Professor Slinz bowed and when his head travelled back to 90 degrees the Glee Team were totally naked.

Belinda spoke first, the lioness leader of the pack she was.

'Professor, we are lowly urchins and you are cleverer than Einstein. Please insert your DNA into us!'

The half moon spectacles of Prof Slinz became foggy with desire. He could feel his little one get a bit bigger inside his undergarments. My it had been a while. Designing market smashing cookware takes a toll on the private life.

Giselle continued

'Yes Mr Proff Proff. Proffer me your sword of enlightenment!'

Slinz gulped. His little rascal was throbbing by now and he thanked all above us all for his long white coat.

Bella finished the three pronged seduction.

'Yes Mr Brain. Let's be havin you!'

That was it. Slinz threw his coat asunder and pulled out his salmon coloured cock. The girls fluttered their eyelashes before pouncing. It wasn't long before the whole factory was a pit of sin.

Belinda was ripping down the overalls of a packaging engineer, sucking and teasing his purposeless nipples. Professor Slinz was licking Giselle's lids spotless and Bella was on her knees clutching for everything she could get. It was a magical environment. The factory had been operating at a high turnover rate and the deliverables had been getting overwhelming. This was just the type of relaxation any business was obliged to provide to the whole team and they were glad of it.

Suddenly, Spooner, bounded into the factory room. 'Did somebody call IT support?' he yelled as he unclasped his braces.

The congregation of orgy participants cheered as he ripped off his clothing. Bella joked at him in between the cocks of Production Director George Macintosh and Neil McDuff from Quality Control:

'Well if we did Spoons we'd be on hold with the helpdesk for three and a half hours waiting to get our issue resolved!' laughed Bella.

'Come here you big breasted beauty. I'll give you a First Contact Resolution alright!' Spoons squeezed in next to McDuff and Macintosh as Bella licked and tickled her way through the trilogy.

By now Belinda was sitting on Slinz's dinky face being aroused by his millions of grey whiskers each with a mind of its own. Giselle was having her way with a burley colander puncher and the visored Helga was cuming in her best Scottish accent. It was a heave ho of bodies and moisture.

But where in the devil's wasp-nest was Maeve?!...

Belinda Blinked;

Chapter 13;

The Wicked-ish Bisch;

Belinda regained her composure. As best she could.

'Good heavens that was a powerful portion of sex. I'm as hot as a half-fucked fox in a forest fire.' she flustered pulling up her thong on the wrong leg.

'Ditto' crooned Spooner.

Belinda looked around at the mess of bodies scattered amongst the pots and the pans. She scrunched down the top of her face.

'Where are my people?'

'Beats me.' yawned the sweaty Bella in-between Neil McDuff's balls.

'Where's Slinz?' Spooner said.

Belinda and Spooner immediately looked at each other's position... and ran.

Belinda and Spoon stormed into the laboratory store room where a body was gagging Prof Slinz with their silken stockings.

'What are you doing?' shouted Belinda.

The body stared up at her from across the floor as cruel as an ice cube.

'Why are you doing this, Mrs Sylvester?' shouted Spooner.

'My name is Giselle Maarschalkerweerd de Klotz. And I am the Special One!'

'Noooooooooooooooooooooo!' yelled Belinda.

'I'm looking after numbero uno, fool. It's over. Time to update your CV Blumenthal.'

Giselle pulled out a mini pistol-gun from the netted band around her thigh, she aimed it at the ceiling. She fired and a barrage of cooking aids fell from the storage racks on the ceiling above them all. They tumbled onto Belinda and Spooner, stopping them in their tracks because they had started running towards the treacherous lady.

Giselle grabbed the hapless Slinz by the armpits, bundled him over her shoulder and staggered out of the sash window with original glassware.

'Shit. Now we're really in the stink hole.' exclaimed Spooner emerging from underneath the heap of toastie makers...

'Giselle...Giselle... oh why did it have to be my best friend?' sobbed Belinda. 'What are we going to do now? she's kidnapped Slinz.'

'There, there Belinda.' purred Spooner as he felt her full ass in his hands.

She turned to face his face and began to kiss his lips, then his nips and then his cockshaft of patriotism. She chewed and choked on it as if it was to be the last time, effervescent with relief from escaping certain death at the hands of her old Glee Team friend Giselle....

6.3 hours later Belinda coolly took the camouflaged leather gloves from the leather room wall and opened up the secret meeting room of Steele's Pots and Pans. She and Spooner walked down the corridor and entered the room. There they all were... her trusted gang of cookware professionals... hand-picked by her and her singularly. Belinda's practiced eyes travelled to each face sat around the space aged reflective table.

Bella; Tony; Sir James; Des and not forgetting Paddy the barman amongst other's serving cold Aussie Chardonnay. All in all there were about nearly 20 individual characters. Belinda stood quietly in front of Sir James's favourite flip chart.

'Greetings colleagues, I have called you here today because I trust in you. As you all know the end is nigh upon us all. If we don't rescue Professor Slinz, this will surely be the end of Steele's Pots and Pans. Maybe even of quality yet affordable cookware anywhere in the western hemisphere.'

Bella burst out a babyesque snotty cry and was comforted by the Duchess's long gloved fingers.

'Yes Bella, these are grave times, but I believe in us. In friendship.... in professional connections... in Steele's Pots and Pans!

The top secret meeting room erupted in cheers.

'We will not go down without a fight! They may have taken our Slinz, but they will never take our pans!'

'Yes! Capital!' shouted Sir James boldly.

'So colleagues, now is the time for action! That is why I, Belinda Blumenthal, International Sales Director, propose we create an underground movement!'

'Hot diggity-dawg!' cooed Jim Stirling not so boldly.

'One, all and everyone, welcome to the first official meeting of the Confidential Order of Cookware Knights…. who's with me?'

One by one the people sat around the table rose to their feet.

'I am!'

'Me!'

'You betcha!'

'Anything for you, boss!'

Belinda beamed;

It was still cold as cold could be in East Berlin. A deranged beating fist banged politely on two huge scale doors somewhere in the depths of a decrepit office block.

'Enter!' wheezed Herr Bisch from behind a cloud of smoke sitting at his desk.

The doors swinged open and in strutted the beautiful form of Giselle clad all in black patent leather.

'Move your sitzfleisch!' shrieked Bisch.

Giselle's steel tipped high heel shoes echoed on the stone slabs as she moved a little quicker to his desk.

'Do you haf ze blueprints my Special Von?' asked Bisch.

'No Herr Bisch I don't.'

'Aaarrrrggghhhhhh,' he screamed. 'It voz that sexy little von voz it not? Vot iz her name?'

'Belinda Blumenthal, Herr Bisch?'

Herr Bisch Blinked;

'But...' began Giselle.

'ZERE IS NO BUT IN BUSINESS!' shrieked Herr Bisch as he rose over his desk and hobbled to his feet.

Giselle Blinked;

She'd never seen her master stand before. It turned out the famous Herr Wolfgang Bisch was a mere 5 foot 1 inches tall. Engulfed with annoyance he took his walking cane and raised it to beat his Special One. But Giselle was too quick for him. She kicked her leg to 90 degrees and pinned Herr Bisch to the grimy office wall with her stiletto.

'But I have one better.' she spoke.

Giselle clicked her fingers. Annoyingly her patent leather gloves didn't allow for much connection and it sounded like a rather pitiful "phat" as opposed to a sharp snap. No matter. Thinking on her mighty fine toes Giselle clapped her hands instead. A couple of henchmen entered the office dragging a big bag of something behind them.

'I have Professor Slinz himself.' she exclaimed.

Giselle unripped the bag and out tumbled the frightened as all hell Professor Slinz. One half of his half-moon spectacles was smashed and he had a few loose bogeys dangling from his nose, obviously from when he'd been crying for mercy inside the bag.

'He's the only one alive who knows the true Tri-Oxy Brillo recipe.' said Giselle as she looked down at him.

Bisch shuffled closer to him so his chin whiskers were itching Slinz's facial skin.

'Ve meet again Herr Slinz. Now you vill tell us everyzink…'

The newly formed Confidential Order of Cookware Knights exited the Steele's Pots and Pans complex and blinking in the sunlight walked to their respective modes of transportation. Tony ambled to his handsome Jaguar; Sir James limped to his groovy Rolls Royce and the Duchess mounted her beautiful horse Toffee Apple Chew.

Just as they did so Maeve from reception ran up to them shouting, no screaming; 'Belinda, Des, Bella, Tony, Patrick, Bill from HR. Be-Jesus, EVERYONE take cover! It's a bomb threat… get behind the cars away from the offices!'

'What the…?' chorused the newly born Confidential Order of Cookware Knights in unison.

Everyone scattered just before a massive explosion ripped through the car park. Tony's Jag had just gone up in smoke. A cacophony of car alarms shrilled all around as the members of The Confidential Order of Cookware Knights lay on the ground bleeding profusely.

Belinda Blinked;

It was just enough to see a hazy figure limping away from the explosion. Then the fearless International Sales Director of Steele's Pots and Pans fell unconscious...

The End;

Wow!!!....

If you enjoyed Belinda Blinked 4; then Belinda Blinked 5; will shorten your life expectancy by at least three (tri) years, so immerse yourself deeper into Belinda's sexual world of betrayal, big..ish business deals and why the rich aristocracy just don't give a fuck... I promise!

Rocky xxx.

But hey... you're still drooling for more then why not let me send you some exclusive Belinda material. I've got some stuff which I didn't have room for in the books and you're welcome to read it. I also sometimes send out a newsletter with info about the main characters, a new book or podcast. It might keep you up to date on the Belinda franchise and whet your appetite for more! Or jus bore you to tears....

It's easy, just email me at flintstonerocky@gmail.com and I'll get back to you.

So this is what you get;

Material that didn't make any of the series....

A copy of Belinda's pay check, only Sir James, Tony and the IRS has this highly classified info!... well perhaps Giselle... and defo Helga...

An occasional newsletter.... like once every 3 years...

Advance notice of what's happening in Belinda's world!... jus read the books...

Myself, Belinda, James Spooner, not Giselle, Bella, Tony and Helga would love you to leave us an honest review. It really helps us to maintain our visibility in the book rankings. Thank you! And if you can do one on iTunes...???

Sir James Godwin couldn't care less.... Hrrmmph;

If you haven't yet read Belinda Blinked 1; 2; 3; they're here!

BB1   http://amzn.to/2njv0Mh

BB2   http://amzn.to/2mQdVvK

BB3   https://amzn.to/2OOlRYs

You can also find us at

www.BelindaBlinked.com

www.RockyFlintstone.com

Or why not purchase the book My Dad Wrote a Porno

http://amzn.to/2mQhWjR

where you'll get lots of extra info on the podcasts!

And I've now got a poster where you can have a personally signed
message from myself... for example...

'To; Ex-wife, Happy f**king birthday you dirty b**ch. -Your ex-husband.

Well maybe not... but you get the idea?? Something nice??

Or enjoy the podcasts... find them on ACast or ITunes goo.gl/XgScSj

Or even splash out on some merchandise.....

www.mydadwroteaporno

Back to Contents

Thx for getting to the ENdddddddd... jus sayin....

Rocky xxx

Printed in Great
Britain
by Amazon